Don't forget!

- Water the plants
- Feed the cat
- Buy toilet paper
- Brush your teeth
- Weed the garden

Have fun! 'Til Monday,
Hugs and kisses,

Mom

This book belongs to:

_____

Be nice to this book!

Library of Congress Cataloging-in-Publication Data
available upon request

First published in English copyright © 1995 Abbeville Press.

Copyright © 1995 Coppenrath Verlag. Story by Christa Wisskirchen.
Illustrations by Annet Rudolph. Translated by Laura Lindgren. All rights reserved
under international copyright conventions. No part of this book may be reproduced or
utilized in any form or by any means, electronic or mechanical, including
photocopying, recording, or by any information storage and retrieval system, without
permission in writing from the publisher. Inquiries should be addressed to Abbeville
Publishing Group, 488 Madison Avenue, New York, N.Y. 10022. The text of this book
was set in Goudy. Printed and bound in China.

ISBN 0-7892-0070-8

First edition
2 4 6 8 10 9 7 5 3 1

TOUGH TIMES FOR FATHER BEAR

By Christa Wisskirchen
Illustrated by Annet Rudolph

Abbeville Press   Publishers
New York   London   Paris

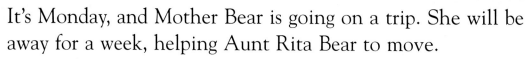

It's Monday, and Mother Bear is going on a trip. She will be away for a week, helping Aunt Rita Bear to move.

"Will you really be all right without me?" she asks.

"Sure," says Father Bear, "it won't be hard! Baby Bear doesn't need a bottle anymore, and Lisa Bear can already tie her shoes, count to thirty, and write her name."

"And what can you do, my dear?" asks Mother Bear.

"Everything, of course!" Father Bear says, laughing.

Mother Bear gives everyone two kisses, but Baby Bear gets three, because he is still so little.

"Good bye, Mother Bear!" they shout.

"What do we do now?" asks Lisa Bear.

"Let's play!" Baby Bear shouts.

"Yes," Father Bear agrees, "let's play at 'shopping.'"

He doesn't know how wonderful the supermarket is to play in: lots of aisles for hide and seek, cans to roll, and people to pester . . . Father Bear has to think hard about everything: where are the toilet paper, noodles, and crackers? And just who put all these bags of candy in the shopping cart?

"Ohhh, this is tough," Father Bear groans. Then he rushes Lisa Bear and Baby Bear to the checkout stand.

How will he feed these hungry bears today? Ah, Lisa Bear's favorite food: spaghetti with—*whoops!* lots of ketchup—even the cat gets some. Father Bear wonders why the ketchup doesn't spread so far when Mother Bear shakes the bottle.

Strange that the spaghetti is sticking in the pot too.

"This is fun!" Baby Bear shouts. "Will you cook French fries tomorrow?"

"Ohhh, this is tough," Father Bear sighs. Then he looks for the paper towels.

On Tuesday they work in the garden. Father Bear brings a big can of paint for the garden wall. Lisa Bear makes sure that everything is a beautiful blue.

"Hey!" Mrs. Bristly Bear yells. "I didn't want to take a shower!"

Who could have turned on the water?

Baby Bear is weeding the garden. But wait, those aren't weeds. Guess what lunch will be today?

"Ohhh, this is tough," Father Bear mutters. Then he cleans the paintbrush and peels twenty-seven carrots.

On Wednesday they go to the amusement park. For the whole day, just like Lisa Bear and Baby Bear have always wanted. Lisa Bear even wins a flower in the ball toss game.

That naughty Baby Bear had better come out of the haunted house right now. The ghosts are scared of him.

And who is left carrying the big prize?

"Ohhh, this is tough," Father Bear groans. Then he lugs the stuffed animal home with them.

They are barely inside their house when it turns pitch black outside and a storm breaks. Lightning flashes and thunder rolls. All the lights go out. Nobody is *afraid* of the thunderstorm. But a little cuddling doesn't hurt.

Father Bear reads the longest good-night story. Soon Lisa Bear and Baby Bear are sleeping, and Father Bear's arm goes to sleep. He can't move in the bed.

"Ohhh, this is tough," Father Bear yawns, then his eyes close too.

On Thursday morning the three Bears look out of the window and say "Uh-oh! It's still raining." They had wanted to go outside. Well, it may be a rainy day, but they'll just have their picnic inside on the rug—milk, juice, honey, bread, salad, and ice cream. Yum!

They decide to play pirates and Indians and to pretend that Father Bear is their prisoner. Pirate Captain Lisa Bear raises the flag, and Chief Baby Bear takes aim.

"Ohhh, this is tough," moans Father Bear. If he moves a muscle, he must face the consequences.

On Friday it's time to do the laundry. Washing clothes is easy, thinks Father Bear. Just put them in the washing machine and let it do the work. But what a surprise when the clothes come out . . . Everything has turned a pretty pink. Baby Bear, which button did you press?

Lisa Bear tries on Mother's favorite blouse. Funny, it fits! She wonders if she got bigger or if the blouse got smaller.

"Ohhh, this *is* tough," growls Father Bear. Then he wonders what to tell Mother Bear.

Evening comes and that means it's bath time.

"Have you scrubbed behind your ears?" Father Bear is about to ask. *Whoops! Splash!* There was something slippery on the floor . . .

"Dad! You've come to play with us!" Lisa Bear yells.

And now they shout and splash and laugh and there's not a dry spot left in the bathroom.

"Ohhh, this is tough," pants Father Bear, and he shakes his wet fur.

On Saturday Lisa Bear says, "Mom's coming back tomorrow!"

They look around and suddenly notice how messy the whole house is. They'll just have to clean up.

Quick! All the toys go into Mother's dresser!

Quick! Vacuum all the rooms.

Uh-oh, the bucket, Baby Bear, watch out! But it's too late.

"Ohhh, this is tough," sighs Father Bear. Somehow the house seems more of a mess than it was when they started.

At night, the lights go out all over town. Lisa Bear and Baby Bear are fast asleep. So who is that zipping around, dusting things around and wiping and scrubbing and cleaning and vacuuming and even baking a cake?

That is Father Bear. There is so much to do, he doesn't even have time to say "Ohhh!" Very late, in the middle of the night, he finally finishes and wearily falls into his bed.

On Sunday, Baby Bear asks for the eleventh time: "When is Mom coming?"

And then they hear *ding dong!* The two Bear children race to the door.

Hooray! Mother Bear is back. Everybody gets lots of hugs and kisses. And who is sitting on the sofa, looking so tired?

"Hello, dear!" says Mother Bear. "Was it tough being without me?"

"Not at all," Father Bear yawns, "not tough at all," and he winks.